WILL NORTHAWAY
AND THE GATHERING STORM

YOUNG AMERICAN PATRIOTS
BOOK FOUR

Will Northaway &
The Gathering Storm

Susan Olasky

CROSSWAY BOOKS

A PUBLISHING MINISTRY OF
GOOD NEWS PUBLISHERS
WHEATON, ILLINOIS

Will Northaway and the Gathering Storm

Copyright © 2005 by Susan Olasky

Published by Crossway Books

   a publishing ministry of Good News Publishers
   1300 Crescent Street
   Wheaton, Illinois 60187

Cover design: David LaPlaca

Cover illustration: Thomas LaPadula

First printing 2005

Printed in the United States of America

Library of Congress Cataloging-in-Publication Data
Olasky, Susan,
 Will Northaway and the gathering storm / Susan Olasky.
  p. cm. (Young American patriots ; bk. 4)
 Summary: No longer indentured, seventeen-year-old Will has spent a year on the Teasdales' farm working and learning to trust God when, in 1769, his old friend Tommy arrives in Boston as a British conscript and asks Will to help him desert.
 ISBN 1-58134-478-3 (TPB)
 1. United States—History—Colonial period, ca. 1600-1775—Juvenile fiction. [1. United States—History—Colonial period, ca. 1600-1775—Fiction. 2. Farm life—Fiction. 3. Soldiers—Fiction. 4. Conduct of life—Fiction. 5. Boston Massacre, 1770—Fiction.] I. Title.
PZ7.O425Wgg 2005
[Fic]—dc22   2005007709

CH		15	14	13	12	11	10	09	08	07	06	05
15	14	13	12	11	10	9	8	7	6	5	4	3	2	1

ONE

Vultures circled overhead, casting threatening shadows on the ground and piercing the morning stillness with their cries. Will Northaway shaded his eyes and squinted toward the hill where he could see several birds hunched over their prey like mourners at a funeral.

Angrily he raised his musket and shot into the air, not expecting to hit one of the birds, but wanting to scare them away. The buzzards on the ground flapped their huge wings and took to the sky to join the others.

Will lowered the gun and trudged up the hill, his thoughts gloomy. A calf was missing, and he feared what he would find. Sun radiated off the parched ground. Everywhere he looked, the ground was dry and riddled with cracks. A year's crops lay withered on the stalk. It was clear that 1769 would be another year of debt and hardship, and hopes for the future were no better.

He reached the crest of the hill and saw the calf. A wolf, he figured, judging from the violence done to it. Will knelt down to examine the body, then stared up at the buzzards still hovering overhead. They'd done damage as well, but Will wasn't going to let them do any more.

He dragged the body, or what was left of it, to a grove of trees. Under the spreading limbs, in the one bit of shade left to him, he buried the calf, using a small axe that he carried to dig out the hole. He piled rocks on top of the shallow grave, brushed off his hands, and stood up.

He'd have to tell Mr. Teasdale about the calf—and he could almost picture the man's disappointment. The loss was another blow for a family that had already suffered its share of hardship.

Will reloaded his musket and set off for the barn. In the distance he could see shirts and handkerchiefs hanging from the clothesline. Betsy had been up early doing the wash in the nearby creek.

How different his life was from six years before, when he'd been a street urchin living in one of London's worst slums. Then he decided to sail to America, working on shipboard to pay for his voyage. Captain Mattison was a good man. In Boston, he found Will a fair master—a printer by the name of Spelman. But after a while, Mr. Spelman returned to England, selling Will's apprentice papers to another printer, John Mein.

As Will thought about his second master, anger and bitterness came rushing back. Mr. Mein's loyalty to the king and his political troublemaking had put both of them in danger. Finally Mein shot a man and had to flee to England. His last act before escaping was to free Will from his indenture.

Will remembered that day well. Freedom! But how would he support himself? He had halfheartedly looked for another printing job, but times were hard in Boston. So many people were out of work that he soon gave up.

When Mr. Teasdale told Will that he could use an extra

pair of hands on the farm, Will accepted. For the past year he'd labored in the fields, earning his red neck and leathered face with long hours in the sun.

He liked working hard. Not a day went by that he wasn't exhausted when he lay down on his cot. He was often too tired to think, and the looming trouble with England seemed far away.

Will looked across at the neighboring farms. Mr. Teasdale's fields were laid out in neat rows hugging the hillsides. Will knew that on the other side of the trees that bordered the farm were more fields, and beyond them even more. It was hard to believe that this whole area had been forest not too long ago. Now farmers were living side by side, with no room to grow.

Will sighed. Maybe he'd be a farmer, maybe a printer—but it was hard to imagine doing either of those things near Boston. He was too poor and the opportunities too few to make a go of it there.

The bell broke into his thoughts. Lunchtime. Will began to lope across the field, grinning at his good fortune. He still hadn't grown accustomed to a real noontime meal that came regular as clockwork.

Betsy Teasdale tended the vegetable gardens near the house. They produced food for the family and for the local market. No matter how bad a season it was for the cash crops—tobacco and corn—the vegetable garden fared well. Chickens scratched among the rows, looking for bugs and worms in the well-turned soil. A pond near the house was home to several ducks and one mean goose.

Will washed up before going inside, where he found Mr. Teasdale waiting at the head of the table.

"Did you find the calf?"

"I found it all right. Dead, up on the hill. I'm thinking it was a wolf that brought him down."

Teasdale frowned. His face was a road map of wrinkles, not from age but from the sun and the cares of the world. His couldn't be an easy life, working a farm and raising three children alone, since his wife's death several years before.

Will could see the disappointment and frustration in his eyes. The children, Betsy and the two younger boys, were silent and stared at their father somewhat fearfully.

Mr. Teasdale smiled then. "Who are we to accept good things from the hand of God and not bad? Blest be the name of the Lord, maker of heaven and earth."

The children nodded as though a decision had been made. And Will realized, as he watched their exchange, that one had been made. The Teasdale family, despite the hardships they faced, would continue to bless God.

During the growing season, lunch was the big meal of the day, meant to fill a farmer's belly so he could go out and work all afternoon. Will filled up on chicken and biscuits, listening with half an ear to Adam and Noah prattle about what they'd done that morning.

"We'll have to set traps."

Will looked up, suddenly realizing that Mr. Teasdale had been talking to him. "Traps?" he repeated.

"Wolves and men don't mix. We'll get McAllister and

the others to lay some traps too. Can't have wolves threatening our livestock."

Will nodded. He didn't know anything about laying traps—but that was the good thing about working for Mr. Teasdale. He'd learn. Suddenly he felt more cheerful. Trapping wolves sounded like fun.

TWO

Farming outside Boston was difficult. The ground was rocky and the growing season short. From time to time Mr. Teasdale heard reports of better land to the west, in Connecticut or even New York. Around the table at night, when the family pondered how many bushels of corn would come to harvest, the farmer talked about moving.

"Sell our land here?" Betsy complained. "Move away?"

"Betsy doesn't want to move because of Micah Walker," Adam snorted. "He's cow-eyed over her." He and Noah made kissy faces at each other.

"Pa, make them stop," Betsy protested, glaring at her little brothers.

Mr. Teasdale glanced sternly at the boys, and their kissy faces were replaced by expressions of angelic innocence.

"Leave your sister alone. You'll appreciate what a blessing she is to us when she's no longer here cooking your meals."

Noah's mouth dropped open, as though he'd never thought about Betsy leaving home. "If she doesn't cook, who will?" he demanded.

"I guess you will," Will said, laughing.

"Uh, uh, not me," the boy protested. "I'll be working too hard in the fields. I'll be exhausted. Adam will have to do it."

Adam shook his head. "I'm joining the army. I'm not cooking for you."

"What army?" Will asked quietly.

"I guess the militia," Adam said. "As soon as I'm old enough, that's what I'm going to do. Betsy will just have to stay home until then. It ain't fittin' for soldiers—or future soldiers—to be cooking."

Betsy stood up and began gathering the plates. Will could tell by the two red circles high on her cheeks that she was angry. The sound of the pewter plates being stacked together was louder than usual.

He sighed. He would have helped her clear the table, but that would embarrass Betsy. She didn't like the men messing in her kitchen.

Sometimes Will felt awkward in the midst of the Teasdales. They treated him like family, but he knew he wasn't really. At some point he'd have to leave. If Betsy married, which was looking likely, perhaps Micah Walker would move out to the farm. Will would surely have to leave then.

When evening came and the sun sank low in the sky, a breeze began to blow. Will and Mr. Teasdale picked up their muskets and headed out, carrying three well-oiled iron leg traps. Each trap opened like a strong jaw that would snap closed when an animal stepped on the trigger.

"Can we come?" Adam and Noah begged.

"No," their father said. "We aren't trying to advertise our presence."

Noah was about to protest, but his older brother poked

him hard in the side and gave him a warning look. Will held back a smile.

The two men, for Will was now a man, hiked up to the hilltop where the calf had been killed. Will pointed out the rocks that marked the animal's grave. From there they could see paths carved into the landscape. They headed down the dry trail that led into the woods. The ground was scuffed bare by different animals traveling the same way, day after day, from watering hole to watering hole.

Mr. Teasdale stopped at one point and bent over. He stood up and looked around, then bent over again. Finally he stood up and nodded. "We'll put one here," he said.

Will tried to see the spot with the farmer's eyes, but to him it looked identical to a dozen other places they'd already passed. He figured he'd ask later, but right then there was work to be done. They couldn't just lay the trap on top of the ground. It needed to be placed right below the surface.

Mr. Teasdale rubbed the jaws of the trap with a grease that he said smelled good to wolves. Then he opened the jaws wide and set the trap in the shallow hole they'd dug. When he was satisfied with its placement, they raked a thin layer of dirt and leaves onto it so that it was well hidden.

Mr. Teasdale hung a strip of cloth from a nearby tree to mark the trap's location, and as they walked away, he wiped his greasy fingers onto the trunk and branches, hoping to attract the wolf's attention.

They repeated this procedure two more times. By the time they were finished it was dark, and they walked by moonlight back to the cabin, careful not to follow the same trail.

"How will other folks know the traps are there?" Will asked.

"It's our land, for one thing," Mr. Teasdale said. "And they'll note the scraps hanging from the trees."

"Have you ever seen a man caught in a trap?"

"I haven't," the farmer said. "But I've heard of it. Those traps could break a man's leg, I suppose."

Will shivered. He'd be more careful walking through the woods than he'd ever been before.

Up ahead a lantern in the window flickered its greeting. Will yawned and realized how tired he was. It had been a long day since finding that calf—he was ready for bed. He said good night to Mr. Teasdale and headed to the barn.

As he settled under his blanket, familiar night noises lured him to the edge of sleep. As he listened to the frogs and katydids singing their night songs, and as the rhythm of his own breathing slowed, Will felt sleep just beyond his grasp.

He'd be moving soon, he could feel it. Ever since he left England he'd not lived very long in any one place. London to Boston, then to Worcester, then back to Boston, and now the farm. He always figured it was his masters' fault that he didn't put down roots. Though he might want a home, God had not yet given him one. As he fell asleep, he dreamed about where he might head next.

THREE

Every few days Will checked the traps. Sometimes he took the smelly grease and rubbed it on the metal, being careful not to touch the trigger. Each time he pictured those metal jaws cracking down, snapping his wrist as if it were a twig, he broke into a cold sweat.

A few of the neighboring farmers had also set out traps, but they had no more success than Will and Mr. Teasdale. They heard occasional reports about missing chickens, but it was more likely a fox was the culprit there.

In October two of the Teasdales' lambs went missing. Will was the first to notice.

"Noah, Adam," he called. "Weren't you supposed to bring the sheep to the pen?"

"We did," the boys insisted in unison.

"We brought 'em last night and put 'em in the pen," Adam added.

"Did you latch the gate?"

"Adam did," Noah replied, pointing at his brother.

"No, you did," Adam answered.

"No, I didn't. I had to go help Betsy carry in the washing before it rained. You said you'd do it."

"Be quiet," Will barked. "I don't care which one of you didn't latch the gate. You must not have even shut it, for two of the lambs are missing. You'd better go hunt for them, or your pa will be furious."

The boys dashed away, still more interested in blaming each other than in finding the animals. They figured the lambs had gotten stuck someplace, because everyone knew sheep were the dumbest animals in the whole world.

They searched all the known danger spots close to the house, continuing their conversation.

"Sheep are dumber than ants!" Adam shouted.

"Dumber than ants? Why, ants ain't dumb," Noah argued. "They're smart and organized like soldiers. No, sheep are dumber than snails."

"Snails are pretty dumb," Adam admitted. "But not as dumb as . . . slugs." He gave his brother a satisfied grin.

"Okay, slugs are dumb, but not as dumb as worms."

"Worms are dumb, but not as dumb as . . ." Adam searched his brain for something dumber than worms, but it seemed as though all the really dumb critters had already been taken. "But not as dumb as . . . *you!*"

Noah humphed and threw a rock at his brother. "Take it back!" he shouted.

"Can't," Adam answered smugly. "It's the truth."

Noah set another flurry of rocks sailing toward his brother.

Adam ducked out of the way. "Bible says so!" he shouted. "It says we are like sheep—and if sheep are so dumb, then I guess we are too." He began to laugh and return fire on his brother. Soon a full-fledged war had broken out, and the search for the missing lambs was forgotten.

Will heard the boys laughing and shouting from behind

the house. He stalked around back and saw them pelting each other with stones.

"Aren't you supposed to be looking for those lambs?"

"Yes," Adam said, putting his remaining stones in his pocket for later. "We're sorry, Will. We got distracted."

Noah tried to match his brother's remorseful expression, but he had a hard time keeping a grin off his face. "I'm sorry too," he said. "We did check all the spots back here. We didn't see any sign of 'em."

Will scowled. "Your father will be back in a little bit, and he's not going to be very happy when he hears how you've been foolin' around."

"But you're not going to tell him, are you?"

Will grumbled something to himself and stalked away, not bothering to answer. He headed out away from the house, keeping his ears cocked for the sound of a lamb in distress. Again he saw a flock of buzzards hovering overhead. He found one nearly-stripped carcass near the pond and another on the edge of the woods.

Maybe the culprit was something other than a wolf, but Will didn't think so. He decided to carry one of the lambs back to the house to show Mr. Teasdale. He took off his vest and wrapped it around the bones to carry them home. Then he buried the other carcass and headed back.

Will was angry. It was such a waste to lose two lambs besides the calf already gone—and this such a hard year.

By the time he reached the cabin, Mr. Teasdale had

returned. He met Will in the front yard. Will held out the carcass.

"I found one of them near the pond and the other near the woods," he said. "Looks like a wolf to me, but I thought you'd want to see."

Mr. Teasdale looked the remains over carefully and nodded. "Didn't see any tracks?"

"Ground's too hard," Will answered. "Didn't see a thing."

Mr. Teasdale nodded. "Keep checkin' those traps."

"I will."

When Will had lived in town it seemed as though no one thought about anything but politics. People were always stirred up about something, whether it was taxes or soldiers or tea. But in the countryside Will learned that many other things were more important. Mr. Teasdale was a patriot, and sometimes at night they talked about politics, but every morning the farmer woke up and scanned the sky for signs of rain. Will often saw him bent over the soil, letting the dry loam trickle through his fingers. Will learned that worrying about politics was a luxury that not everyone could afford.

In a way he was relieved. He liked the rhythm of the farm. "Six days you shall labor and do all your work," was more than a verse in the Bible, he discovered. And even on the Lord's Day, which the Teasdales always marked by going to church, the cows had to be milked and the animals fed.

But sometimes Will felt stranded. He itched for excitement and remembered with longing previous autumns in Boston. The farm wasn't that far from Boston, two miles or so, but it was on the other side of the Charles River and going there meant crossing the river and circling the long way around to Boston Neck. The road to Cambridge was easier, and that's where the Teasdales went to church.

One day he was carrying water for Betsy's garden. The lettuce and beans were gone, but turnips, squash, and pumpkins were still growing.

"When will you harvest this stuff?" he asked, pointing at the sprawling plants.

"We'll go to market in two weeks," Betsy said. "We've got to finish picking the apples, and Pa wants to slaughter a pig or two."

"I hope I'll get to go."

"Of course you will," Betsy laughed. "We all go. It's a real festive time."

"I sometimes miss the city," he said softly.

"I didn't think I'd ever hear you say that," Betsy said. "Haven't you seen enough riots to last a lifetime?"

"But I think all of that has passed over," Will said. "I don't think there's nearly as much tension as there used to be."

Betsy yanked on a turnip, shook the dirt off of it, and stuck it in her basket. "You are so dumb, Will Northaway. The only reason things seem better is because you're living on a farm, not in the middle of town."

"But don't you think we'd hear about it if there was trouble?"

"I'm not saying there has been trouble, but it's brewing. Pa says it's as bad as it's ever been. I hope that nothing happens before we go to market."

Will agreed, but not for the same reason. Betsy, he figured, wanted to avoid the action—and he didn't want to miss it.

FOUR

The unearthly whine set Will's hair on edge. He froze and looked around, not sure what he'd see. He'd been checking the traps since daybreak, and as usual hadn't found anything. He was retracing his steps when he heard the sound.

He crept forward, cringing as the dry leaves crunched underfoot. He'd never take a critter by surprise if he kept making so much noise. The trap lay ahead, and though Will had already checked it once that morning, he felt a flutter of excitement.

He raised his musket to his shoulder and continued on. The whining grew louder, broken up by snapping and snarling. Will's finger quivered on the musket's trigger as he broke through into the clearing where the last trap lay buried under the leaves.

A hound puppy, caught in the trap's metal jaw, bared its teeth at Will before turning to snarl at the heavy clamp around its leg. Will lowered the musket and stepped forward, but the hound lowered its ears and growled. Will stopped. He didn't want to shoot the dog. But if he did nothing, the dog would die anyway.

He squatted down and began speaking softly to it. "Good puppy. Shh. Shh. It's okay."

The dog continued growling, stopping only long enough

to snarl and snap at its leg. It couldn't seem to make up its mind which was the worst threat, Will or the trap.

Will continued to talk in a soothing voice, all the while inching forward. He'd put the musket down, so he could extend his hands and show the dog he meant no harm.

The dog acted crazy, snapping and growling and foaming at the mouth. Will figured it was because of the pain caused by the trap, but he couldn't be sure. He didn't want the dog to bite him. He could feel his heart pounding as he slowly reached out his arm, thinking that if the hound had a chance to smell him maybe he'd calm down. But the dog seemed even more riled up.

Will looked around, hoping for an idea. When he eyed the branches of a nearby tree, it came to him. He'd need someone to help, but he thought he knew how to untangle that hound.

Will bounded to his feet and picked up his musket. He trotted over the fields toward the house, where he hoped to find Noah or Adam. But the boys were gone with their father somewhere, and only Betsy was home.

Will shouted at her. "Come with me! It's an emergency."

Betsy put her hands on her hips and said, "I've got work to do. Who'll do it if I don't?"

"There's a dog caught in the trap," he explained, coming closer. "I need help if I'm going to free it."

Betsy sighed. "You'll have to kill it anyway. Once its leg is all torn up, you'll have to shoot it. It's the only kind thing."

"Would you be quiet and come?" he begged, wishing

heartily that Noah or Adam would appear. The boys wouldn't ask questions.

When Betsy hesitated, he grabbed her arm and pulled. "Can you run dressed like that?" He scowled at her long skirts.

Betsy gave Will a disgusted glance and dashed off the porch. He easily caught up to her and pointed in the direction of the trap. When they were almost there, he held out his hand for Betsy to stop.

"Here's my plan," he said. "We'll cut a branch about five feet long. It has to have a forked end. I'll trim the two branches of the fork, and then you'll hold the dog's neck down while I release its leg."

Betsy began to protest, but when she saw Will's determined expression, she held her tongue. It couldn't hurt to try, she guessed.

Will had already spotted the limb he had in mind. He'd brought a small axe with him, and he began to cut the branch. Once he'd separated the limb from the tree, he trimmed it so that it would suit his plan. Betsy watched carefully.

"This should work," he said. "The trap's just over that hill. You can hear the dog whining." They stopped, and Betsy heard the pitiful yelps.

"Poor puppy," she said.

"Let's go," he answered, dragging the branch behind him. "Just move real slowly near him. He's likely to bite."

The dog had tired himself somewhat, but when he saw Betsy and Will he began growling again.

"He's just afraid we'll hurt him," Will said.

"I know that," Betsy snapped. "Hand me the branch."

She lowered it so the forked end was facing the creature. Then she moved the branch forward. The dog snarled and began to snap at it.

"You're going to have to distract him," Betsy said. "Maybe if you poke him with a stick from the other side."

Will fetched a long straight stick and circled around the dog. Then he squatted down and slid the stick toward it. The hound lunged and grabbed a mouthful of stick. While he was trying to wrest it away from Will, Betsy extended her branch over the dog's neck and pinned him to the ground.

"I've got him," she squealed. "Hurry up. I don't know how long I can hold him."

The dog tried to wiggle free, but Betsy held the stick steady. Meanwhile Will rushed over to the trap and pried its jaws open. The crushed leg came free, and Will set the bloody trap on the ground.

"Here's the tricky part," he said. "I didn't really think about what we'd do next. If you let the dog go, he might bite us or run off. Then he'll die."

"I can't stand here all day while you figure it out, Will Northaway."

Will's face was creased with concentration. Finally he said, "I think I've got a plan. If you take off your apron, we can throw it over the dog and carry him back to the house using the apron as a sack."

Using one hand, Betsy untied the apron and tossed it to Will. "This had better work," she said.

Will held the apron open and inched toward the puppy,

which was straining to get at its leg. Once Will had the apron in place, he yelled for Betsy to lift the stick. As she did so, he pulled the apron under the dog's head and caught both ends near the tail. The dog was so startled at first that it didn't fight. Only when Will had it firmly wrapped up did it begin to struggle.

Betsy carried the musket and axe while Will lugged the dog home. By the time they arrived, Mr. Teasdale was back with the boys.

"Where have you been?" he asked.

"Will saved a hound that was caught in one of the traps," Betsy eagerly explained. "I had to help."

"Can I see him?" Adam begged.

"We have to figure out where to put him. He's hurt and angry, so you'd better stay away."

"I'll get a rope," Noah offered. "You can tie him to the porch."

"And I'll get a box with a blanket," Adam said. "He'll sleep in it." The two boys ran off.

Meanwhile Betsy said, "I'll get him some food. That'll be the easiest way to let him know that you mean him no harm."

"Maybe a pan of water," Will added, and Betsy nodded before heading inside.

Will slipped the rope around the dog's neck, and Betsy tied the other end to the porch railing. Only then did he set the dog down and pull off the apron.

The hound immediately began licking its leg and whining. But soon it smelled the food and dared to take a bite. Then it drank a little water. The family stood in a circle, watching the puppy slowly relax. No one tried to touch it or get a better look at the leg. That could come later. They watched as the dog crept into the box. It scratched at the blanket until it was arranged properly, then went to sleep.

FIVE

The hound puppy was tough. The trap hadn't broken the leg, just mangled the skin and muscle. They cleaned it with rum, rubbed it with a salve made of medicinal herbs, and wrapped it with a bandage.

Each day the dog seemed stronger. It began getting up from its bed and following Adam and Noah around the garden and out to the pond. The boys threw sticks and tried to get the dog to chase them, but it would flop down in the grass and refuse to move. Still, they adored the puppy and were seldom seen apart from it.

Adam insisted on calling the puppy Soldier, so Will grew accustomed to the two younger boys barking out orders: "Sit, Soldier." "Stay, Soldier."

The following days threw the whole household into turmoil as everyone prepared for the Boston market. The Teasdales loaded everything into the wagon: bushels of apples and potatoes, pumpkins and squash, jars of honey and jelly. Betsy had spent summer evenings spinning yarn, which she added to the load. Straw brooms with twig handles stood upright in a barrel.

When the wagon was ready, Mr. Teasdale lashed a tarp over it, took his seat at the front, and urged the team of oxen forward. Will and the boys walked alongside, followed by Soldier.

"If he gets tired, I'll carry him," Adam promised.

"You couldn't carry that dog ten feet," Noah said.

"There's room in the wagon if he gets tired," Betsy said from her perch next to her father. "Stop bickering."

It was a late Indian summer day. The air was crisp, and a cloudless blue sky arched overhead, providing a perfect backdrop for the golden leaves that clung to the oak trees along the way.

When they reached Boston, Mr. Teasdale drove the wagon to the common, where other farmers had already claimed spots. Fall market days were festive occasions. Busy farmers, who rarely took time during planting and harvesting seasons to come to town, gathered to exchange news and catch up on family gossip. Betsy flitted from wagon to wagon greeting her friends, and the boys took Soldier to explore the town.

Will surveyed the scene. Brightly colored quilts hung from lines stretched from wagon to wagon. The air smelled of apples and smoke. Across from Boston Common, the tent city housing British soldiers had disappeared. Will set off to explore, wondering how else the city had changed since the last time he was here.

First he headed over to see Mrs. Simpson, feeling it was his duty to see how she was faring. She ran a boarding house, and Will had stayed there when he first came to Boston and was apprenticed to her brother, Mr. Spelman.

He hadn't even reached the front steps when the door flew open and Jacob Simpson flew out. "Guess who's home?" he screamed, throwing himself at Will. "Sam's home. He came home last week, and he'll be here all winter."

Will's face lit up. Sam, the oldest of the three Simpson brothers and his best friend, had been at sea for the past two years. "Where is he?" He pushed past Jacob and bounded into the house.

Sam ambled to his feet, a big grin spreading across his face when he saw Will. "Well, look who's here," he said, grasping Will in a big bear hug. "I'd have come out to the farm, but Ma won't let me out of her sight. She's afraid I'll slip off to sea again."

"I guess she's trying to fatten you up," Will said, noticing how thin his friend had become. "You look like you'd blow away in a storm."

"No one ever got fat eatin' Cook's food. You remember. But I'm not starvin', though it is good to be home and have some home cooking for a change."

He smiled at his mother, who was beaming at him. Will thought Mrs. Simpson looked years younger than the last time he'd seen her.

Sam bounced nervously on the balls of his feet. "Let's go for a walk," he said. "I'm not used to four walls and a roof. I'm about to go crazy." He pulled on a coat and pushed Will to the door, barely letting his friend say good-bye.

Once they were down the street, he slowed down. "It's hard being back," he said. "Ma seems so old and tired, and the boys are hard on her. Plus this city feels like it's going to explode. I'd forgotten how tense things were— and now with soldiers everywhere. I won't be surprised if there's shooting."

Will was surprised by his friend's comments. "Do you really think it's that bad?" he asked. "Maybe I've been on the farm too long, but I thought things had quieted down. Of course, maybe that's because I'm no longer working for John Mein."

"I heard he had to run away to England."

"He shot a man and beat up Mr. Gill. By the time he fled, he'd made enemies of every patriot in Boston. When I worked for him, I would have agreed that things were bad. But it looked quiet enough on the common. If there are soldiers everywhere, where are they staying? The tent city is gone."

"A lot of 'em are staying with Tories. And even patriots are lodging them for the money it brings in. But Ma says the boys Jacob's age go around taunting the soldiers. They think it's great fun to hurl oyster shells at them. They've even surrounded them and pushed them off bridges. Did you hear about John Rowe?"

When Will shook his head, Sam continued with his story. "He has a daughter who's been seen with a naval officer, but Mr. Rowe claims to be a patriot. Ever since the soldiers have been here, he's been swept up in their parties—and apparently having a good time. But one day he was having dinner in a tavern, and an officer said to him, 'I expected you to be hanged before now, for you deserve it.' Ma says he was so upset by the officer's joke that he rushed home to his wife and has been afraid to go out since."

Will and Sam laughed at the image of Mr. Rowe huddling in his kitchen for fear of the rope. But then Sam grew serious.

"It's bad in England," he said. "They're impressing boys off the street and forcing them into the navy."

"I heard they tried that here," Will said. "The citizens rescued the poor lad, and the soldiers haven't done it since. They'd be fools to try."

"Ma says more than thirty soldiers deserted in the first weeks they were here. The Brits were lazy about tracking them down, so those boys are probably in New York by now. What do you think they'd do if they caught 'em?"

"Shoot 'em, I expect. Otherwise they'd have no soldiers except the officers—and everyone knows officers won't fight."

Will and Sam walked in friendly silence until they reached the waterfront and the row of small shops and taverns that faced it. A band of grubby redcoats, whose uniforms looked as though they could use a good washing and mending, spilled onto the cobblestone street. Will and Sam pushed through the crowd, ignoring the grumbling and muttered oaths thrown at them.

"Watch where yer goin'." A couple of soldiers stepped in front of them to block their way.

Will stopped and rolled his eyes. "I'm not looking for trouble," he said.

"But maybe it's looking for you."

The other soldiers laughed.

Sam smiled back, but the soldiers had turned sullen. The two friends suddenly realized that what they did next could result in major trouble.

"Come on, Will," Sam said. "We can get a drink somewhere else. These lads don't even seem to recognize that you're a landsman of theirs."

"I guess not," Will said. "Six years have washed the English out of me."

Suddenly a soldier who'd been leaning against the tavern, listening to the conversation but not taking part, stood up and shoved his way to the center. His uniform looked newer than the others, or better cared for anyway. He eyed Will curiously and said, "What's your name?"

Will shoved his hands in his pockets and stared at the soldier. "What's yours?"

"Tommy Fenlaw."

"Tommy Fenlaw." Will said the name slowly, letting it roll off his tongue. He was certain he'd heard it before. Suddenly he remembered, and a grin split his face. "Tommy Fenlaw!" he said again, grabbing the British soldier by both arms. "How are you, and what are you doing dressed like that?"

The soldier grinned. "I thought it was you," Tommy answered. "Though you were a tad scrawnier when I first saw you in Rotherhithe. Boy, it's good to see you."

Sam and the other redcoats watched the scene with amazed expressions.

When Will saw Sam's confusion, he explained. "When I was just a street lad in London, I got into some trouble with . . ." He looked around at the soldiers and shrugged. "With some redcoats. I ran away to escape my punishment, and Tommy here rescued me. He cleaned me up and introduced me to his father, who knew Captain Graham. If it weren't for Tommy, I'd probably be dead."

"Join us for a drink?" Sam asked.

Tommy looked at his fellow soldiers and shrugged.

"Sure. Though I might be causing trouble for you. It doesn't seem like the folks in Boston welcome us."

"We're not worried about it," Will said. "Come on."

The trio was met by strange glances as they walked down the street, but Will hardly noticed. He hadn't felt so happy in a long time.

SIX

"How did you get here?" Will demanded, once he, Sam, and Tommy had reached an inn where they could talk without being disturbed.

Tommy shook his head. "It's a long story, and not one I'm very proud of," he said.

The boys waited while Tommy took a drink and collected his thoughts. "For a while now it's been hard for the king to recruit enough soldiers. The pay is bad and living conditions are poor. All you have to do is look around Boston, and you'll see what I mean. Half the boys in red don't get enough to eat, though our officers are doing fine. That's why you see them hanging around the ropewalks, begging for jobs."

Will scowled. "I've heard they'll work for anything."

"Well, so would you if you were bored and starving." Tommy held up his hand against their protests. "I know they're taking jobs from Boston men, but they don't have much choice, do they? Anyway, that's not what I want to tell you." He turned and looked at Will. "After Father helped you get on Mr. Mattison's ship, I began begging to go. Father and Mother wouldn't hear of it—and I was angry."

Sam nodded. "My ma was the same way before I ran away to sea."

"I didn't run away, for I feared God too much to do

that. But I began taking long rambles, just enough to worry them—and I guess I hoped that I'd be caught by soldiers and impressed into service."

"So what happened?" Will demanded, leaning forward to hear above the din of voices.

"Exactly what I hoped. I was caught and forced into the king's service. At least they let me go home—accompanied by a guard, of course—so that I could say good-bye."

"Couldn't your pa do anything?" Will asked.

"Nothing," Tommy said, shaking his head for emphasis. "He didn't have the money for bribes, if that's what you mean."

Tommy was quiet for a minute, fighting manfully to hold back any sign of emotion, but Will could tell it took an effort.

"Last thing I saw was Ma weeping into a handkerchief, with the little ones clinging to her skirts. It's not a scene I'll soon forget."

"How long ago?" Will asked.

"It's coming on two years since I've seen them."

Sam scratched his head. "Did I hear you say something about Mr. Mattison?"

"Sure. He's my uncle, my mother's brother. He's the one who took on Will here. He's the one I wanted to go asea with, but Ma wouldn't have any of it."

Sam grinned. "This is a small world. Your uncle is here in Boston, staying at my ma's house, like he always does when he's in town."

"Really?" Tommy eyed Sam skeptically.

But when Will nodded agreement, Tommy's doubt melted away. "Will you take me to him?" he begged.

"Sure, but he's probably at the common for market day. Can you get away?"

Tommy glanced at the clock on the mantel above the fire and nodded. "I've got a couple of hours yet." He stood up and tapped his foot impatiently as the other boys finished their drinks and stood to go.

The market was crowded with farm carts and people. Children rolled hoops and tossed horseshoes and rings in the open areas while men and women crowded around the wagons, buying and selling and exchanging news. Will, Tommy, and Sam pushed through the crowd until they found Mrs. Simpson, who was examining brooms with a well-practiced eye.

"Ma, have you seen Mr. Mattison?" Sam asked.

"Not for the past half hour. I saw a knot of men smoking pipes and talking politics over that way—perhaps he's there."

The boys set out in the direction pointed out by Sam's mother and eventually found Captain Mattison in the middle of a debate about taxation. Will wasn't surprised to find Mr. Teasdale there as well.

The sea captain, who seemed to be listening more than talking, saw Sam and nodded. He glanced at Will and Tommy, at first without recognition. Then he looked again, and a surprised expression crossed his face. He leapt to his feet and rushed over to them.

"Will Northaway!" he said, slapping the boy on the

back. "You have grown up." Then, turning to Tommy dressed in his red uniform, he frowned. "Tommy?"

Tommy couldn't hold back his excitement any longer. "Uncle John," he said, throwing his arms around the sea captain.

Captain Mattison's frown deepened. "What are you doing dressed like that? You aren't in the army?"

"For the past two years," he admitted with a mixture of pride and embarrassment.

"But why? This isn't our fight."

Tommy stepped back, his face almost as bright as his uniform. "Don't scold me," he hissed. "Don't you think I regret it every day I'm here? But what's done is done. I don't have much choice in the matter."

Captain Mattison allowed himself to smile. "This isn't the time for harsh words. Forgive me." When Tommy nodded, the sea captain smiled more broadly. "Let's get away from this crowd. It's fun for an old salt to listen to these arguments, but I'd much rather hear what you've been doing."

They made an odd sight strolling down the crowded Boston streets, with Tommy in his red uniform and Captain Mattison dressed as the merchant ship captain he was. When they stood side by side, the resemblance between them was obvious.

Sam and Will hung back while Tommy and his uncle walked ahead. Finally the young soldier became aware of the time. He hurriedly said his good-byes before rushing back to his unit.

A few minutes later Captain Mattison excused himself

and headed off, leaving Will and Sam to speculate about where he was going. The boys wandered back to the market, where farmers were packing up and some were heading home. Will found Mr. Teasdale and got permission to stay with Sam for the night.

Again Will noticed how the city had changed. Soldiers were everywhere. They lived in the ropewalks and Faneuil Hall and private homes throughout the city. Their cannons were set up in the square, aimed toward the Customs House. No matter where Sam and Will walked, redcoats were coming out of taverns, going into houses, and walking down the street. But Will saw no large public demonstrations against the British.

The two friends stopped when they saw a group of soldiers in front of them.

"Watch them," Sam said. "See those boys lurking over there? There'll be a row."

Will watched curiously as the Boston boys strolled forward, their hands shoved in their coat pockets. The soldiers looked up. When they saw the boys, they shouted insults at them. The Boston boys pulled broken oyster shells out of their pockets and hurled them at the soldiers before dashing away down a narrow alley.

The soldiers gave halfhearted chase before quitting. One reached up and wiped a trail of blood from his cheek, where a sharp shell had cut him.

Sam and Will turned away, not wanting to face the soldiers' anger. "Those kids know the soldiers can't shoot; so they pester them whenever they can."

"But what if one does shoot?" Will asked.

"Then we'll have trouble. Up to now, it's just worry."

"I guess that's better than rioting all the time," Will said. "Remember when they destroyed Lt. Governor Hutchinson's house?"

"No one's going to do that with so many soldiers around," Sam said. "Even the customs agents feel safe now. All those officials who fled to Castle Island think the soldiers have brought peace. They're moving back."

"Right here in town?"

"No. They're still too frightened for that. But they're buying land outside of town and building big houses, surrounded by guards."

"What does your mother think?"

"She does the washing for some pretty important families. You wouldn't believe how many people are trying to straddle the fence. They're going to dances with the British officers while swearing their love for Sam Adams."

"And what does Sam Adams say?"

"He thinks the British are nothing but trouble and bad for the city. You'll see tomorrow that the Brits don't darken the doorway of the church. They'll be doin' the same things on the Sabbath that they do on any other day. That drives Sam Adams crazy."

Will frowned. "It's like I live in a different world now," he said. "We hardly think about the British. In fact, what I think about most is how I'm going to trap a wolf."

And Will proceeded to tell Sam what he planned to do next.

SEVEN

Will had wolf on the brain. He'd talked to Mr. Teasdale and other farmers and discovered that not that many wolves still lived around Boston. They'd been trapped and hunted until they didn't pose much threat. But that didn't make the farmers any fonder of them. A man could still earn a bounty for any wolf head he turned in.

Will liked the idea of a bounty. He didn't have any money, and trapping that wolf seemed a good way to get some.

Mr. Teasdale had told him it was unusual for a wolf to bother livestock. It was also unusual for a wolf to kill more than it could eat. Will's wolf seemed to be doing both things—and maybe that meant something. The more Will thought about it, the more certain he was that his wolf was a loner. If he'd been traveling with a pack, they would have stripped all the flesh off the bones of the calf and the lamb rather than leaving half the carcasses behind.

Now that the harvest was done, Will had time to devote to the problem. He set out one frozen day to talk to the neighboring farmers.

"I'm Mr. Teasdale's hand," he said when a burly man answered the first door.

The farmhouse was warm and inviting. The man asked Will in to sit in front of the fire, where he was mending a yoke.

"I'm wondering if you've lost any livestock to wolves?" Will asked.

"No. I haven't, but you might ask Mr. Chalmers down thataway," he said, pointing down the hill. "I heard he lost his milk cow."

After thanking the neighbor, Will rushed off. He had a lot of territory to cover if he wanted to discover how far the wolf ranged.

Mr. Chalmers was a gruff old man who acted as though Will was to blame for the loss of his cow. He didn't know what had happened to it. Probably someone had stolen it, he said. But when Will pressed, the man finally let him in the house and called his eldest son, a boy about twelve, to answer Will's questions.

"Do you remember when your cow went missing?"

"Nope," the farmer grunted.

"Sure you do, Pa," the boy interrupted. "It was right before the harvest moon."

Will was excited, hearing that. It would have been about a week after he'd lost the lambs. "Didn't you notice any trace of it?"

The boy scowled at his father. "Pa was so certain that the Davises had stolen it, he never would look. Exceptin' of course, that we went over to the Davises and asked 'em. They denied takin' the cow—and we didn't see her anywhere."

Will eyed Mr. Chalmers curiously. "Why'd you think the Davises took your cow?"

"'Cause they're lazy and no account," he said. "It seemed like something they'd do—and I'm still not convinced they don't have her hidden away. They knew she was a good milker."

"Oh, Pa!" the boy said with exasperation. "She hasn't been a good milker for years. She was old and scrawny and about dried up."

Will could tell that Mr. Chalmers regretted calling the boy over. He stood up and buttoned his coat, preparing to leave. "Thanks for your help. If you lose any other livestock, would you let Mr. Teasdale know?"

The boy nodded while his dad just gave a grunt.

Will was glad to leave that farm. The sagging fences and ill-kept vegetable garden should have warned him that Mr. Chalmers was no kind of farmer.

But Will didn't know what to think about the cow. Stolen or eaten by a wolf? He shrugged and continued on to the next farm.

By the end of the day his feet were frozen and his hands so stiff he could hardly uncurl them. When he reached the Teasdale farm and pushed open the heavy wood door, it was suppertime. A duck was roasting in the fire, its skin crackling and spitting.

"That sure smells good, Betsy."

"It'll be ready soon," she said. "Pa's in the barn."

Will kept his coat on and headed around to the barn. He found Mr. Teasdale mucking out the stable.

"So what did you discover?"

"I must have gone ten miles around," Will said. "The Chalmerses' cow was the largest animal to be missing, but they don't know what happened to it. But other farmers reported three sheep and two goats and even a couple of geese missing. They figured a fox could have taken the birds, but the goats and sheep were pretty big for that."

"Have they set out traps?"

"Some have. Some were just too busy with the harvest to do anything." Will's face turned thoughtful. "It's going to be hard to catch this wolf. His range is big, and between us we have so many animals—he can just pick 'em off one by one."

"That's so," Mr. Teasdale agreed. "Except with winter comin' we'll be keeping our livestock closer to home. He's going to find it harder to isolate the weak and the young."

"Does that mean ignore him and hope he moves on?"

Mr. Teasdale hung the big pitchfork with his other tools and brushed off his hands. "I don't think so. If we don't kill him now, he'll be troubling us in the springtime. Now that he's had a taste of livestock rather than game, I don't think we'll be rid of him."

Over dinner they continued talking about the wolf. Even after Bible reading and prayer, Will had a hard time getting the killer out of his head. As he went to sleep that night, his dreams were full of yellow-eyed wolves, chasing and nipping at him, so close that he could smell the musky odor rising from their shaggy coats.

The next morning, an hour before dawn, Will packed a rucksack with food and water, pulled on heavy leather boots, buttoned his thick overcoat, yanked on a broad-brimmed hat, and set out to catch the predator. During the night he'd come up with a plan. He grabbed the musket off the wall and let the door shut quietly behind him.

Soft flurries fluttered to the ground, but the air was too warm for snow. Will walked surefootedly to the pen outside the barn where the sheep were huddled. They *baaed* as he pushed through them until he came to one of the lambs. He looped a rope around its neck and led it away. At first the lamb struggled against the rope, but before long it was trotting willingly behind Will as he cut across the frozen stubble toward the woods that bordered the small farm.

They'd laid the traps on an animal trail and caught nothing. Now Will was going to use a different kind of bait. When he reached the trap, he tied the loose end of the rope to a tree, careful to make sure the lamb could not reach the trap when it came to the end of its tether. The lamb baaed mournfully, but Will ignored it.

Will chipped at the frozen ground until he'd dug up the first trap. He wiped it well with the grease that Mr. Teasdale had used. Then he reburied it under a shallow layer of dirt and leaves. He repeated the process at the other two traps. He wiped the smelly grease on trees and leaves, hoping it would cover his own scent. Then he returned to the lamb, which had gotten tangled in the rope. Will shook his head, muttered a few words about how dumb sheep are, and untangled the lamb. Then he spread some oats on the ground before heading to a hiding place he'd spotted last time he'd tended the traps.

There was nothing more to do but wait.

EIGHT

Tommy Fenlaw peered out the window of Faneuil Hall, where he was quartered, and groaned. The sky was gray. Low clouds blocked the weak winter sun. He longed to curl up under his stiff woolen blanket and go back to sleep. For a second he closed his eyes and indulged his wish, but then the door flew open, and he heard the heavy footfall of boots.

Tommy hopped out of bed and pulled on his own boots, rushing to make himself presentable before the officer reached his bunk. All around him soldiers were pulling themselves together as the boots clomped closer. "Yessir. Morning, sir." By the time the officer reached Tommy, the lad was ready with a stiff salute and "Sir."

He relaxed as the officer passed by, glad to have escaped a flogging. The officers were quick to make examples of their unwilling young recruits, trying to whip them into shape. But it was a hard battle. Boston was a miserable city, the townsfolk resented the soldiers, and for long stretches of time the soldiers had nothing to do.

For Tommy, used to the comforts of home and the warm companionship of his family, it was worse. He was lonely, and the hours stretched painfully before him. He longed for something worthwhile to do.

As soon as he was free, he headed away from his fellow soldiers and their complaints. He was drawn to the waterfront, which felt as much like home as anyplace. Tommy had grown up on the water—the River Thames in England—and he never tired of the bustle and the watermen's gossip. His uniform made him stand out and put a barrier between him and the local workers. But once he got them talking, most were willing to overlook his clothes and odd accent.

That day Tommy had decided to ask for work. He'd become friendly with some folks in one of the ropewalks, and he figured if he could work some he could make a little money, keep warm, and pass the time.

He pushed open the door to the ropewalks and found the owner. "Could I work for you?" he asked.

Garret Pine scowled. "You'd be bringing me nothing but trouble," he said.

"But I'd work hard. You know I'm strong, and I've been doing this kind of work all my life."

"It ain't you, Tommy. You're worth three of these louts. But they'd start doing mischief against me for hiring a lobsterback."

Tommy scowled. "You can tell 'em I'd toss off this uniform in a second, if I could."

"I wouldn't say that out loud. If your officers get wind of that sort of talk, they'll be worried about you deserting. They'll flog you to get the notion out of your head."

"I'm not planning to desert. I just want to work. I'm tired of being hungry all the time, and I'm tired of standing around. I'm almost hopin' for trouble so we'll have something to do."

Mr. Pine shrugged. "You're welcome to be here, and you can work all you want. I can feed you, but I can't pay you."

Now it was Tommy's turn to scowl. "You'd be takin' advantage of me."

"Look, lad, I'm not willing to disrupt my shop by hiring a lobsterback. Business ain't that good—and when I need to pay cash money for a worker, I'll hire a local. I won't apologize for that. But if you want to be here, work, and eat something besides what they're feeding you, you're welcome. Or you can look elsewhere."

The conversation had been going on while the men were on a break, smoking their pipes outside so as not to risk fire. But now the door opened, and slowly they began to trickle in, eyeing Tommy curiously. Over the past several months they'd come to know the lanky soldier. They didn't seem to mind him hanging around.

Tommy scanned their familiar faces. He'd chosen this particular rope factory because the owner and workers were decent folks. Now he had to decide. Work a little here and hope that eventually he could get paid, or work elsewhere and not know what kind of trouble he'd find.

Always in the back of his mind was a fear of attack. He was used to the occasional rock or rude remark thrown at him by rowdy boys. But sometimes the hostility seemed as though it might boil over into violence, and when it did, Tommy didn't want to be on the wrong end of a musket.

The men went back to work, and the owner waited for Tommy to decide.

"I'll come whenever I can," he said. "Eventually you'll see that I'm worth a wage."

Tommy took off his coat and joined the other men working the cranks and pulleys to twist the fiber into strong ropes for Boston's fleet of ships. The fact that the boy wasn't being paid became widely known. Most of the workers shrugged as though it didn't matter to them as long as their own jobs weren't affected.

But friends of some unemployed men grumbled. They figured if Tommy weren't working for free, Garrett Pine would have to hire one of the men who loitered on the wharf all day, drinking ale and causing trouble.

Tommy didn't let their dislike bother him. He enjoyed working, and went to the ropewalk whenever he could. He almost felt like a local—and once he took off his red coat he looked like one too.

NINE

If Will hoped his plan for trapping the wolf would work quickly, he was disappointed. Each day he spent hours in his hidey-hole watching the lamb tied to the tree.

"I should give up," he complained to Mr. Teasdale one day, after several hours of watching.

The farmer laughed. "You're learning patience and perseverance," he said. "A wolf has a huge range. You can't expect it to wander by just because you've set a trap."

"I'm not known for my patience." Will gritted his teeth. "Maybe it's dead, and I'm wasting my time."

"Jake Allen came by today to say he'd lost a goat. He followed tracks in the snow and is convinced it's a wolf. Allen just lives three miles over."

Will sighed. He'd been setting the trap every chance he had, but now snow had come, and he wasn't looking forward to long hours in the cold.

Just then Betsy announced dinner. She took a pot of steaming chicken stew off the hook over the fire and set it on the scarred table.

"That smells good," Mr. Teasdale said, smiling affectionately at his daughter. "What will I do if you marry that fellow in town?"

Betsy blushed bright red and began fussing over the biscuits. "Hush, Pa. He hasn't said a word . . ."

To ease the situation, Will looked up from his stew and asked, "Do you know how to cook wolf? I'm planning on bringing one home tomorrow."

"How many times have I heard that?" Betsy asked. "In any case, I'm not cookin' or eating wolf."

"If we were hungry enough you would," Adam piped up.

"I don't think we'll ever be hungry enough to eat wolf."

"I don't think Will will ever be lucky enough to trap one," Noah added.

During the night more snow fell; so by morning a fresh three inches covered the ground. Will pulled two sweaters on under his coat and stuffed a couple of roasted potatoes in his pocket to eat during the day. He didn't need water—melted snow would do.

"I'm off," he announced. "Wish me well."

"Will you be back tonight?"

"I'm taking a blanket and I might stay out," he warned. "Don't worry about me." Will fetched a sled from the barn and piled his blanket and other supplies on it. Then he fetched the bait, a goat this time, and headed out.

The farmhouse soon disappeared from Will's sight as he trudged through the snow, half dragging, half carrying the struggling goat. When he finally reached the place where he'd decided to set his trap, he again tied the animal to a tree. Then with a pine branch he brushed the snow, wiping out his footprints, and hid himself well under an outcropping of rock.

The hours crept by. Will wrapped the blanket tightly around him and wished he could light a fire. Every so often he took a nibble from one of his potatoes, now cold, or gnawed on a piece of jerky. He felt sorry for the goat, bleating pitifully in the cold.

Will felt himself nod off, and he jerked himself awake. The sun was low in the winter sky. He scooped a handful of snow into his mouth and waited.

An owl hooted overhead. Will was getting impatient. He was about to scramble out of his hiding place when he heard a howl. He froze and ducked back under the outcropping. He felt for his musket. Then, leaning back against the rock, gun pointed at the goat, he waited.

The howl broke the stillness again—closer this time. Will felt the hairs on the back of his neck tingle. If he'd been a dog, he thought, his hackles would be up.

The goat scrambled to its feet and pulled against the tether, bleating frantically. Will saw it stop and sniff the air before tugging once again at the rope.

Will was so tense his hand ached where it gripped the musket. He swore he could hear his heart pound in his chest and feared for a minute that the wolf could hear it too. The next howl sounded so close that Will almost jumped. He willed himself not to move, not to do anything to scare the animal away. Then he saw it.

The wolf was smaller than he expected, not much bigger than a medium-sized dog. Its head was huge and its legs long in comparison to its body. It was covered with a thick, shaggy, grayish-blackish coat. It stood perfectly motionless uphill from the lamb, its ears twitching and nose testing the air.

Will thought it too far for a good shot, though his hand

trembled on the trigger. *Come on, come on,* he coaxed in his mind.

Mr. Teasdale had told Will that wolves hunt on the run, preferring to chase their prey, overtake it, and attack from the face. The farmer had once seen a pack of wolves take down an elk that way. Still, Will was unprepared for the wolf's speed when it began running toward the goat.

The goat pulled vainly against the rope. Will aimed the musket, forcing himself to wait—but knowing that if he waited too long, the goat would be dead. The wolf's sharp teeth would make quick work of the animal.

Steady, steady, he cautioned himself as the wolf approached. The goat arched its back and lunged just as Will pulled the trigger. The musket roared. It kicked back, knocking him off balance. He threw an arm out to catch himself.

Through the haze of smoke from the musket, Will saw the wolf sprawled out, its blood turning the snow from white to red. The goat had been knocked to its side and was trapped under the wolf's body.

Will crept forward to make sure the animal was truly dead and not just stunned. He stretched the musket out before him and rolled the wolf over until the place where the musket ball had entered became visible. Amazingly, he'd shot it in the chest. Will sighed and felt suddenly weak-kneed. Then he saw the goat struggling to free itself. Will untied its rope and led it away.

After he'd retied the goat, Will went back to the wolf. With his hunting knife he cut the animal's head off, for someone had told him that hanging the wolf's head from a post would ward off other predators. He didn't know if it was true, but he was taking no chances. Then he skinned the beast, leaving the carcass for the birds and other scavengers to eat. He was glad he'd brought the sled. He wrapped the head and skin in his blanket, trying not think about Betsy's reaction, and loaded it on. Then he tied the goat to the back of the sled and headed home, tired, cold, and well satisfied with his long day's labor.

TEN

It didn't take Tommy Fenlaw long to figure out that people hated and despised his uniform and not him. When he wore his red coat, he felt eyes burning through him. He was a target for boys with snowballs and could count on being shoved and jostled as he walked down the street.

Sam Simpson gave him some old clothes that he wore at the ropewalk, and before long it seemed that most of the men had forgotten where he came from and why they had any reason to resent him. Even Garrett Pine had forgotten why he was not paying wages to his newest worker. Much to Tommy's surprise, one day the owner paid him as he paid the other men.

That's when Tommy began to hatch his plot to desert. He didn't spend time struggling over his decision. The choice seemed simple—he hadn't chosen to fight in the king's army, he'd been snatched off the street and forced into the uniform. He intended to abandon it as soon as he could, and he thought he had allies to help him.

In some ways travel was easier in winter than summer. When the Charles River froze, the crossing, which could take hours in the summer, was as easy as strapping on a pair of snowshoes. After a snow, a person could even ride a horse across the river.

One day Mr. Teasdale sent Will into Boston for some medicine. Will had just tethered the horse when he ran into Tommy outside the alchemist. Will was surprised to see his friend wearing regular clothes.

"I didn't recognize you dressed like that," he said.

"I'm getting into practice." Tommy smiled. "One of these days I'm going to toss off the king's coat and run away."

Will thought his friend was joking, and he played along. But when he realized Tommy was serious, he grew sober. "If they catch you, they'll execute you," he warned. "Why not wait out this trouble? Maybe there won't be any fighting."

"It's not the fighting I'm afraid of," Tommy said. "But I'm not fighting for the king. What kind of country is it where they can pluck you off the street and force you to fight?"

The two friends walked along, each deep in his own thoughts. Will had struggled for years before crossing over to the patriot side, and he couldn't understand how Tommy could decide so quickly.

"What about your parents?"

"Deserting the army doesn't mean I don't care about my parents. It means I won't fight for the king. Besides, if my father could afford it, I think he'd come to Boston himself." Tommy paused for a second, then continued, "Perhaps it was a good thing the king's men kidnapped me. My voyage, at least, was free."

Will turned and faced his friend. "Don't do anything rash. There's no need to hurry—this present tension will blow off, and you'll be headed back to London and your folks."

Tommy shook his head. "I don't think so. I think one of these days something's going to blow up—and I want to be on the right side when it does." Now it was Tommy's turn to demand something from Will. "When I'm ready, will you help me?"

Will had been expecting the question—and he hesitated a minute. He knew that if it were easy to desert, the British army would have disappeared. But spies and Tories lurked everywhere, ready and eager to turn over deserters to the British. If Will encouraged him, and Tommy was caught and hanged, Will would never forgive himself.

He looked up at Tommy and nodded. "If you're certain you want to do this, I'll help. But you have to listen to my advice. I don't want you running off half-cocked."

Tommy gave a sigh of relief and realized he'd been holding his breath, waiting for Will's reply. "I promise not to do anything stupid," he said.

When the bell on the church tower struck the hour, Will realized he had to head back. "I'll talk to Mr. Teasdale and figure out a plan," he said. "Remember, don't do anything foolish."

By the time Will reached the farm, it was nearly dark. The horse picked its way across the frozen snow, which crunched underfoot. Its pace picked up as it neared home. Will tipped his broad-brimmed hat at the bare branches of the tree where he'd hung the wolf's head—a warning to any other predator that threatened the farm.

He wished the threat of the British army was as easy to overcome as a lone wolf—but the gunships anchored in the bay represented a danger much darker and more powerful.

ELEVEN

Mr. Teasdale agreed to come with Will to town to meet Tommy and talk. He was a cautious man, and Will thought he might convince his friend to stay in the army rather than risk getting caught as a deserter. At least that's what Will was praying. He thought Mr. Teasdale might remind Tommy of his father. They both had a steady way about them.

They met at a tavern that was frequented by all kinds of people, soldiers and citizens alike. In the middle of the day the place was crowded. A fire roared in the fireplace, pewter tankards clanked against the table, men argued, and the sound level crept ever louder as folks competed to be heard above the din.

Tommy was sitting alone at a table in the corner when Will and Mr. Teasdale arrived. They stomped the snow off their boots, adding to the puddle of water on the floor, and took off their hats. Mr. Teasdale nodded at friends as he pushed his way through the crowd, with Will following.

After introductions were made and food ordered, the three settled onto their benches and began to talk. They kept their voices low, bending their heads close in order to hear.

Mr. Teasdale studied Tommy closely. "Tell me about yourself," he said to the boy.

Tommy related his history while Mr. Teasdale nodded, interrupting occasionally to ask a question. It didn't take long before the two were talking about London, ships, and the Bible. It didn't seem to matter what topic came up, Tommy and Mr. Teasdale each had something to say.

As Will listened, he began to grow uneasy. His knee bounced nervously under the table. Finally he could stand it no longer. "Why don't you tell him that deserting is too dangerous?" he demanded.

Mr. Teasdale turned calmly toward his farmhand. "It's not my business to tell him that. He knows the risk—and the reward. I think a man ought to believe in the cause for which he's fighting and possibly risking his life. That's a matter of conscience, between a man and God, and I won't presume to interfere."

"But I don't understand how he'll do it," Will continued.

His friend slammed his tankard down, so that some of the liquid splashed on the table. "Don't talk to Mr. Teasdale as though I'm not here or am too stupid to take part in this discussion. It's my life, Will. Just as it was your life when you chose to come to America."

Will paused and regarded his friend, who was dressed in his red uniform, his hair pulled back neatly in a tail. "I'm sorry, Tommy. But look around. Right here in this tavern there are men who would be glad to gain favor with your officers by turning you in."

"I'm not going to give them that chance," Tommy said. "We're going to come up with such a good plan that I'll slip away. That's what you can help me do—come up with a plan."

All three of them became thoughtful as they considered the task. They were silent as the tavern keeper brought their food and refilled their tankards. Finally Mr. Teasdale spoke.

"Come springtime, folks will be leaving these parts to move to Connecticut and New York. If you can get to the farm, I will gladly fix you up with one of those families. They'll be looking for strong hands to help with the cattle and provide protection against enemies."

Will could tell Tommy was excited by the glint in his eye and the way his hand started strumming on the table.

"I'd need a gun," he said.

"That's right. You don't want to take anything that belongs to the king. Will tells me you already have clothes—some cast-offs of Samuel Simpson." He looked at Tommy for confirmation. "Do you have any money?"

Tommy shook his head. "I've been working a little bit at the ropewalk. Sometimes Mr. Pine pays me."

"Save what you can—and I'll try to find you a gun," Mr. Teasdale said. "Meanwhile, be quiet about what you're thinking. Don't talk to anyone, not even Sam Simpson."

Will stared at Mr. Teasdale. "Sam? You can't think that he'd turn on Tommy!"

"I've heard enough stories about Sam and the spots he's gotten himself in. If it were my life, I'd not want to count on Sam to keep me safe."

Will began to protest. "But that was before he went to sea. I'd be the first to admit that he did some stupid things back during the Stamp Act riots. But he's changed."

"I'm sure he has changed, but I don't think he's ready to bear the responsibility of a secret."

Will wasn't content with the farmer's advice. One cold winter morning he set off to find Mr. Mattison, confident that the sea captain would oppose his nephew's plan. The *Ana Eliza* was anchored in the bay, and Will suspected he'd find Mr. Mattison either on the ship or somewhere close by.

Will started in the taverns, sail shops, and ropewalks, but when he didn't find him there, he prowled the wharf until he found a waterman willing to row him out to the ship.

The wind was icy off the water. Pelicans flew in a line just inches over the surface. Will breathed in the familiar odors: tar, wet wood, salt brine, and fish. It was a heady mixture and brought with it a mountain of memories. Soon the small boat pulled alongside the ship. Will climbed the rope ladder, remembering the first time he'd ever mounted it.

He found Captain Mattison in his cabin, poring over his log. Sea captains wrote down everything, and the ship's log contained a complete record of every voyage. At the sound of Will's footsteps, the captain looked up. He smiled and beckoned the young man to join him. A sailor brought Will a cup of tea.

"You're not honoring the boycott?" Will asked.

The captain shook his head. "I'm a British merchant ship. I make my money, or at least I used to, bringing in tea."

"Has Tommy told you what he plans to do?"

"I hardly see the lad."

"He's planning to desert." Will hoped his words would shock the captain, and he wasn't disappointed.

"Desert? He's told you that?"

"Me and Mr. Teasdale."

"That foolish boy!" Mr. Mattison was furious. "He should have talked to me. I'm his family."

Will was feeling some satisfaction at the captain's response. But he also felt uneasy going behind Mr. Teasdale's back. "I told him it was too risky," Will said. "If they find out, they'll hang him as an example."

"Don't you think I know that? Why would he confide in a total stranger like that Teasdale fellow?"

Now it was Will's turn to be surprised. "He couldn't have told a more trustworthy man," Will said. "I'd trust my life to him any time."

"Then what bothers you about it?" The captain watched Will carefully.

"I'm afraid for him," Will said, as if the answer was obvious. "It's risky."

"Would you say danger is a reason not to take action?"

Will thought about it. "No."

"Do you think deserting is wrong?"

"No. It was wrong for the king's men to kidnap him and force him to serve."

"I agree. If Tommy is a slave—forced to serve against his will—shouldn't we help to free him?"

"Will you take him to London on your ship?"

"If it were up to me, I'd love to have him. But he'd never be safe in London. You know that."

Will sighed. "But what if I help and it goes wrong?"

"God will be with him in danger or in health. Trust Him to do what's right."

TWELVE

The Customs House stood alone at the spot where Cornhill and King Streets merged. Before the British came, merchants filled the bottom floor, while upstairs judges and other colonial officials had their offices. When the redcoats came, they pushed out the merchants and quartered soldiers in their place. Outside on the square, they set up cannons aimed at the Customs House—a bold reminder that the king's long arm stretched all the way to Boston.

British soldiers stood sentinel outside the building, bayonets fixed to their muskets. If the Governor's Council wanted to meet, the councilors had to pass by British soldiers. If a man had business in court, he had to pass a sentinel who would demand to know his business.

Tommy hated sentry duty, but most of his fellow redcoats liked it. They enjoyed the power their guns and bayonets gave them. Since officers were quartered all over town, and since each officer had a sentry outside his lodging place, citizens were stopped throughout the city, at all hours, and forced at bayonet point to say where they were going and why.

Resentment against the soldiers grew throughout the long winter. Short days with little sunshine always made people cranky, but having soldiers in Boston increased the strain. After a day's patrolling, when the redcoats returned to their quarters, they complained bitterly about their treatment.

"I'm tired of putting up with those hooligans," one soldier complained. "They shoved me right off the bridge and into Mill Pond."

"What did you do?"

"What could I do? They ran off before I could climb out. I almost froze to death."

"They'll get theirs," another chimed in. "One of these days an officer is going to give the order to fire."

Tommy pushed through the huddle of soldiers. "I wouldn't be so eager to pull the trigger," he said. "If we start things, they'll want to finish them."

"How can they expect to fight against the king's army?"

"Maybe it makes no sense," Tommy admitted. "But they've got guns, and they know how to shoot them. I bet they even have stockpiles of ammunition. I'd not be in a rush to fight."

"You sound like you know an awful lot about these rabble-rousers." The soldier eyed Tommy suspiciously.

Tommy stared back, daring him to say more. Both stood with hands clenched, eager to fight. But another soldier stepped between them. "Let's save our fists for the Yanks," he said. "We'll need all our energy and anger to take them on."

Tommy stomped over to his bunk, scolding himself for speaking out. It wouldn't do for other soldiers to be suspicious of him. They'd start watching him, and he'd never escape.

Tommy had just come off sentry duty one day in late February of 1770. It had been a hard day of duty. He'd probably been hit with five ice balls, the last one smacking him square in the face. It had taken all his self-control to keep from fighting back. All he wanted to do when he got off duty was to walk as far as he could from the Customs House.

He was walking along when he saw a group of school-children gathering under the Liberty Tree. When they spotted him they began to lob snowballs at him.

"What are you doing?" he asked in his deepest, most intimidating voice.

"Go away, you lobsterback."

Tommy noticed that the children were hiding things behind their backs. He pointed his musket at them. "I bet you've been stealing something. What is it? Come on, show it."

One of the younger boys began to cry. "It's only some eggifies."

"Eggifies?" Tommy tried not to laugh. "You mean effigies. Why didn't you just say dummies? And who are these effigies of?"

One of the older boys smashed his hand across the little boy's mouth. "Keep still. You want to get us all into trouble?"

Tommy laughed again. "You won't get into trouble. At least not from me. Come on, let me see."

The boys pulled out four poorly made effigies, thrown together from whatever cast-off clothes the boys could gather.

Tommy took his time studying them. "Good thing you named them," he said, pointing to the hand-lettered signs that dangled from their necks. "Otherwise no one would know who they are."

"They're merchants who broke the boycott," the little boy said. "Everyone knows that."

Tommy watched as the boys strung them from the tree and took their turns knocking them around. As a crowd gathered, Tommy drifted away, wishing he'd taken time to change out of his uniform. He hadn't gone more than twenty yards when he heard loud shouts coming from behind him. He turned in time to see an older man pulling at the effigies. He was screaming at the children and trying his best to tear all the figures down. When he spotted Tommy, he shouted at him to come help, but Tommy pretended not to hear and continued walking away.

The gathered crowd saw what was going on and began to chase the man through the streets. They ran past Tommy, screaming, "You're a traitor, Ebenezer Richardson."

Richardson turned abruptly, and the crowd followed. Tommy darted down an alley just in time to see the man duck into a clapboard house. When he disappeared within, a few people drifted away. But most of the crowd stayed and continued cursing him. The schoolchildren began pelting his house with rocks. One rock sailed through the window.

Suddenly Mr. Richardson appeared in the opening with a musket in his hand. "You hit my wife with that rock!" he cried angrily, as he pointed the gun out the window.

Tommy heard one of the bystanders yelling, "He's got a gun!" Then another man yelled, "Let's tear the place down."

The crowd surged toward the front door. Poor Mr.

Richardson had probably just hoped to scare them away with his musket. But when the crowd kept pushing against his door until it broke from its hinges, he fired. Immediately people began screaming and streaming away from the house. But one boy—Tommy later learned his name was Christopher Seider, age eleven—was hit by eleven pellets in his chest and died immediately. Another boy was wounded.

The people stared with dismay at the two bodies crumpled on the frozen ground. They gathered them up and carried their limp forms to their families.

When the crowd had gone, Tommy could still see Richardson through a window, holding his frightened wife. He heard the next day that later that night, under cover of darkness, they had escaped to Castle Island.

THIRTEEN

More than two thousand people took part in a procession to honor Christopher Seider. Sam Adams, John Hancock, John Adams, and Paul Revere—all the most famous patriots were there. They used the tragedy to rouse the citizens of Boston against the British. "If this can happen to a young boy," they said, "it might happen to you, or your wife, or your children." Suddenly no one felt safe.

Tommy was desperate to leave Boston. The tension had grown so great that he no longer felt safe walking down the street. He didn't mind the snowballs. He didn't even mind the pushing and shoving. But he feared that under their winter coats, many men and boys might be carrying a musket or a knife.

Tommy knew he wasn't alone in his fear. At the barracks soldiers talked about it all the time. They were nervous—and Tommy knew that nervous soldiers tended to be trigger-happy.

Even the ropewalks no longer felt like a refuge. Four days after the funeral of Christopher Seider, a fellow soldier came to Pine's ropewalk looking for work. Tommy looked up and saw the fellow in his bright red coat—and he knew it meant trouble.

"We don't like redcoats," one of the workers yelled. "Go back to England."

A rope maker pushed through the factory. "Go clean the outhouse if you want to work."

The other workers laughed, but the soldier wasn't amused. He slugged the fellow who'd insulted him, and the next thing Tommy knew, the whole shop had quit work and were beating the soldier. Tommy slipped away before they could come after him.

The soldier finally escaped from the rope makers. He fetched his friends, and they went back to the factory and took up the fight. Later, in the barracks, the soldiers bragged about the damage they'd done to the rope makers. But Tommy doubted their stories. Judging from the cuts and bruises suffered by the soldiers, the Boston rope makers had bested them.

That night it began to snow. It snowed on and off for three days until by March 5 a foot of it lay on the ground. But the snow did not cool off tempers.

The next trouble began simply with a soldier who failed to pay a barber for his wig. The barber complained, and before long the matter was no longer a simple dispute between a storekeeper and a customer. A mob of boys attacked the soldier to force him to pay his debt.

When word of that assault spread to the soldier's friends, they came to his defense. One soldier battered a young man with the butt of his musket. The crowd grew. Young men and boys surrounded the two soldiers, taunting them and throwing snow and ice balls at them before moving on to the Customs House, where they found another target.

A soldier stood sentry there. It was an important post

because inside the building the king's taxes and duties were stored. At first the boys were content to throw snowballs. But as the crowd grew—reaching two hundred or more—the guard began to fear for his safety. He thought about running. But if he did, no one would be left to guard the king's treasury. So he stayed at his post, screaming for help.

Other soldiers, including Tommy, heard his cries. He was coming back from the ropewalks, where he had spent the afternoon. He was dressed in civilian clothes, as had become his habit. Tommy reached the square as his commander, Captain Preston, was marching a small group of men from the barracks to the Customs House.

The crowd was nervous. The funeral of young Christopher Seider was still fresh in their minds.

Tommy stood on the outskirts of the crowd, his tricorner hat pulled low on his head. He hoped the darkness would conceal him from his captain. When he saw the soldiers coming, he was tempted to flee. But something held him in place. He watched as the redcoats marched in formation down the street, their footfall muffled by the snow, and took positions in the square.

The townspeople threw rocks and snowballs at the soldiers. Tommy could hear voices yelling. He even heard someone yell "Fire!" or was it someone saying, "I dare you to fire"?

For a while it seemed as though the standoff would come to a peaceful end. Surely the soldiers wouldn't respond to snowballs with musket balls. But as Tommy watched, his dismay grew. The soldiers, men he'd considered his friends, raised their muskets and pointed them into the crowd.

He heard Captain Preston urge the crowd to go home, but no one moved. "Go on home!" he yelled again, using his bayonet to push his way deeper into the crowd.

A flurry of snowballs, rocks, and oyster shells flew through the air. From where Tommy stood, the redcoats seemed trapped in a sea of hostile men. The yelling grew louder until it was impossible to know who was yelling what. Someone else shouted "Fire." The next thing Tommy knew, one of his fellow soldiers took aim and fired into the crowd. A man fell to the ground. Immediately more shots followed. When the shooting stopped, eleven bodies littered the ground, staining the snow with their blood.

Four men died that night, including a freed slave and a sailor named Crispus Attucks. He was hit in the chest by several musket balls. Seven men were injured, and one of those died the next day.

Tommy panicked. Though he'd promised to wait before deserting, he swore at that moment that he'd never go back to his unit. He strapped on a pair of snowshoes and slipped away under cover of darkness, confident that no one would look for him that night.

FOURTEEN

Will was up early milking the cow when he spotted something staggering through the snow in the distance. The object was dark against the moonlit surface. Will watched for a minute, wondering what creature would be foolish enough to be out in such weather. Then the ache in his own hands brought him back to business. He puffed warm air on his palms before getting back to work.

A half hour later, when he was leaving the barn, he looked out again. This time the figure was much closer and clearly human. Its movements were slow and jerky, like a marionette on a string. Several times the person tumbled into the snow and took forever to right himself. Will paused before setting down the pail. Then he strapped on his snowshoes and set off across the field.

When Will reached the fellow, he had fallen once more. This time he didn't get up, and Will feared he might be dead. He bent over the limp figure, which was dressed only in a tunic and light jacket. Then he rolled the man over and looked upon the ghostly pale face of Tommy.

Will pulled his friend upright and half carried, half dragged his body across the field to the house. He unlatched the door and stumbled through, dropping his burden on the threshold and gasping to catch his breath.

Betsy looked up from the fire. "What on earth?"

"Come help me," Will said. "I found him floundering in the snow. He's half frozen. . . . I don't know, maybe he's dead."

"Who is it?"

Will's throat thickened. "It's my friend Tommy."

Betsy bustled to his side. She bent down over the body and pressed her cheek to Tommy's breast. "There's a heartbeat. He's alive. Let's carry him to the fire."

Together they dragged him to the hearth in front of the fire. Betsy fetched a blanket and turned away as Will removed Tommy's frozen clothes and wrapped him tightly in the wool. Slowly a bit of color began to return to his face.

Betsy sighed. "Why was he out in this weather dressed like that?"

Will, who had been gazing intently at his friend and silently mouthing a prayer, looked up at Betsy. "I thought I was looking at his corpse."

"What is he doing here?" she asked.

"And where's his uniform?" Will muttered.

Just then Mr. Teasdale entered the room. Once Will explained the situation, Mr. Teasdale took charge, setting Betsy to work brewing a pot of precious tea they had on hand for emergencies. She added a generous amount of molasses to the tea and spooned it into Tommy's mouth.

Meanwhile Will heated bricks in the fire. When they were hot, he wrapped them in cloth and set them near Tommy's feet. Then he sat near him on the floor, waiting for him to give some sign of life. Will leaned over, whispering his friend's name.

Tommy groaned. His face grimaced in pain. Finally his eyes fluttered open. When he saw Will's anxious face hovering over him, a weak grin flitted over his face. "I guess I found it," he whispered.

Will snorted with relief. "I found you," he said. "You'd still be stumbling around outside if it weren't for me."

"No matter. I'm found—I prayed I would be."

"What are you doing here?" Will demanded, his voice thickened with emotion.

"I've left," Tommy croaked.

"Shhh. Let him be, Will." Betsy shooed him away and took her place by Tommy's side. "No more talking. You're to have some tea and rest. You can talk and scold later."

Will was not in a mood to be put off. "You don't understand, Betsy. He's deserted the king's army. They may be looking for him at this very minute."

Tommy's eyes opened once again. "It's you who doesn't understand, Will. Something terrible happened last night. They won't be looking for me."

"Why? What did you do?"

"It's not what I did." Tommy's words came slowly, as if they were painful to say. He stared past Will at the clock on the wall. "There was shooting. I saw the bodies on the ground."

"Soldiers?"

"No. Townspeople."

"How did it happen?"

Tommy's eyes closed. His breathing became slow and regular.

"Let him sleep," Betsy said. "You can't do anything about it now."

"I can go and find out what happened," he said. "I'll talk to your father. Unless he forbids it, I'm going into town."

FIFTEEN

Will was anxious to head to Boston to find out what he could, but the melting snow made travel difficult. Mr. Teasdale urged patience. He needed to go to town soon to buy seed, and he'd take Will then.

Five days passed before they could make the trip. On that day, Tommy begged to go with them. He walked with a slight limp and suffered from a cough, but otherwise he'd recovered and was tired of waiting. Though Will stressed the danger and argued against it, Tommy persisted, arguing that he wanted to get advice from his uncle, Captain Mattison.

Mr. Teasdale and Will finally agreed. Dressed in Will's clothes, with a tri-corner hat pulled down on his head, Tommy would blend in with all the other lads who filled the streets of Boston.

The first thing they noticed upon reaching town was the absence of British soldiers. They'd become so accustomed to seeing the red-clad figures marching on the common and lounging outside the taverns that their absence was shocking.

"Where have the soldiers gone?" Tommy asked.

"We'll find out," Mr. Teasdale answered.

"I'm going to Sam's," Will said. "He'll know the gossip, and Tommy can see his uncle."

Mr. Teasdale nodded reluctantly. "Be careful," he urged. "I'll see you back here at two o'clock."

The boys nodded. That would give them several hours to visit with Sam and Mr. Mattison.

They were quiet as they trudged over the slushy cobble-stones to the Simpsons' house. Anytime Tommy's voice rose, Will shushed him. "They'll hear your accent," he warned. "Be quiet."

Tommy nodded grimly. He seemed resentful of the warnings, though he knew Will meant them for his own good.

"I can see I won't be able to stay here," Tommy said. "I'll never blend in. I'll always be afraid."

"But you could move west where no one knows you," Will said. "You don't have to go back to England. That would be foolishness."

When they reached the Simpsons' house, Will urged Tommy to stay outside. "I'll go and see if your uncle is here. That way Sam and his brothers won't see you."

"You don't really believe that Sam would harm me, do you?"

"No, of course not. But it doesn't hurt to be cautious. Besides, his younger brothers do talk—you'll want to avoid them."

Tommy agreed. He waited on the corner, kicking at a tuft of grass peeking through the snow and thinking through what he'd say to his uncle. His stomach fluttered. Would Mr. Mattison think his impulsive decision to desert on the night of the massacre a mistake?

Meanwhile, Will had stepped into an argument. Sam was yelling at his mother about going into town for a demonstration of some kind.

"You aren't going," Mrs. Simpson said, her arms folded across her chest. "You're staying here where I can see you."

"You can't keep me locked up like a child," Sam yelled back. "I'm not a boy any longer."

His mother frowned. Tears welled up in her eyes, but she blinked them back. Then she saw Will. She turned gratefully to him, saying, "You tell him, Will. It isn't safe out there."

Will took off his hat and nodded a greeting at his friend. "What's wrong?"

"I'll tell you what's wrong," Mrs. Simpson said. "Last week some rabble-rousers went down to the courthouse and started a fight with the soldiers. They threw rocks, snowballs, and trash. They taunted them. They urged them to shoot. At some point a soldier aimed his gun and pulled the trigger. Now five are dead and six more injured, and Sam Adams hopes to use the tragedy to start a war. The Boston Massacre, he calls it." She slammed a pan down on the table and glared at the two young men.

Will shrugged. "Where are the soldiers now?"

"What do you mean?" she asked.

"They're gone. I saw not a single redcoat as I rode through town."

"They must have fled to Castle Island—or to their ships. We showed them!" Sam said.

Mrs. Simpson glared at her son. "That kind of talk is what led to the massacre. You boys couldn't leave those soldiers alone. I'm fortunate not to be one of those mothers who just buried a son."

"Mother!" Sam spoke sharply. "You're not thinking

right. Those boys weren't provoking the soldiers for no reason. One of the lads had been stabbed earlier in the day. Soldiers pricked passers-by with their bayonets. They tried to force innocent people from the streets, as though the streets belonged to them and not to the citizens of Boston. Why can't you see that the soldiers brought the trouble on themselves?"

Will interrupted. "Mrs. Simpson, I'm starving. Do you have something to eat?" He wasn't that hungry, but he knew that his question would turn her attention to her duties as a hostess, and he was right. As she bustled about getting food, he asked for Mr. Mattison.

"I think he's upstairs writing," she said. "Sam, go fetch the captain."

Sam gave a noisy sigh and went off. Will ate the thick sandwich Mrs. Simpson prepared for him. Soon he heard heavy footsteps clomping down the stairs, and Captain Mattison entered the kitchen. Will sprang to his feet and shook the captain's hand. As he drew near, he whispered to him that Tommy was outside.

The captain's eyes registered surprise, but he said nothing. He grabbed a coat from a hook and said, "I'm sorry to run off like this, Will, but I need a bit of fresh air. I've been writing all morning."

Will nodded and watched as the door shut behind him. Then he looked up at Sam and asked, "Were you there at the massacre?"

Sam fidgeted awkwardly, glancing nervously at his mother's back.

Will stuffed the last piece of bread into his mouth. He

chewed it deliberately and then said, "Mrs. Simpson, let Sam come out with me. I'll keep a good eye on him."

She nodded. "I'll hold you to your word."

The two friends walked to the Customs House and stood silently on the square. Then Sam described what had happened. His account was similar to Tommy's, though they disagreed about who gave the order to fire. The melting snow had washed away any traces of blood, but it couldn't remove the eerie thought that they stood at a place where men had died violently.

A small crowd had gathered on the square. Everyone was talking about the massacre and the events that followed.

Will turned to a man nearby. "I live on a farm and missed the news. Tell me what happened."

"Miserable lobsterbacks." The man spat onto the cobblestone. "That Captain Preston can claim his innocence until the cows come home, but that don't make it so."

"What do you mean? Did he order them to shoot?"

"That's what I say." He looked ready to fight with anyone who disagreed, but another old man interrupted him.

"Oh, Henry. You know folks disagree about that. Some say we dared them to shoot. Others say he told his men, 'Don't fire.' But I've heard some people swear that he yelled, 'Fire!'

"I guess it would be hard to know who was yelling what," Will said. "It must have been confusing. I remember that night when Mackintosh so riled up the crowd on Pope's Day. It was as if we were different people, not bound by ordinary rules."

Sam swung around and stared at Will. "This is different," he said. "There were armed soldiers here and defense-less people. These deaths weren't accidental. Someone aimed a loaded musket into the crowd and fired. Not once. Not twice. But at least a dozen times."

Will sighed. "You're right," he said. Then he remembered that he wasn't supposed to know that Tommy had deserted; so he said, "What about Tommy? Have you seen him since the massacre?"

"I'm sure he's in the barracks with the rest of them. I hope he wasn't one of the shooters. Though if he was, he should hang."

There was a murmur of agreement. Anyone found guilty should hang. The conversation moved on from the massacre to the funerals and town meeting that had followed. All the prominent patriots had marched in the funeral procession, their sorrowful expressions seen by everyone.

Later that afternoon, Bostonians had held a town meeting, in which they demanded that the British troops leave Boston. At first the British agreed to remove one regiment. But Sam Adams, full of righteous indignation over the massacre, went back to the meeting and gave a fiery address, rousing the patriots to stand up to the British.

The old men standing on the square, telling Will their account, laughed when they described the final showdown between Sam Adams and the governor, Thomas Hutchinson. Adams reminded the governor that three thousand townspeople packed the Old South Church, townspeople who only that morning had buried five of their own—killed by British bullets.

Thomas Hutchinson remembered what a mob could do.

His own house had been destroyed by one several years earlier. He backed down, as Adams knew he would. He promised that as soon as possible, all the British soldiers would board their ships and sail to Castle Island in the Bay.

Adams had later described the governor's reaction: "I thought I saw his face grow pale, and I enjoyed the sight."

As Will listened to the retelling and looked around, he realized that the redcoats had kept their word. They were nowhere to be seen.

SIXTEEN

Tommy and Captain Mattison walked several miles, wrestling with questions about the deserter's future.

"You could get me a job on another ship," Tommy said. "I wouldn't have to go back to England."

"But, Tommy," his uncle said, "the British navy impresses sailors from merchant ships across the seas. You can't escape the long arm of the navy."

"What if I say I'm a colonial?"

"You speak English—the king's tongue—which makes you an Englishman in his eyes. He believes once an Englishman, always an Englishman."

"Then I'll have to go west," Tommy said. "I'm not sure the farming life is for me, but what choice do I have?"

Mr. Mattison nodded. He promised to come up with some money to help Tommy start fresh. When the clock struck the hour, Tommy realized that he had better head back to meet Mr. Teasdale. He said good-bye to his uncle and hurried off. He was nearly to the meeting place when he remembered that the owner of the rope factory still owed him money. Now that he was going west, he'd need every cent he could muster.

Tommy detoured to the wharf. He sauntered to the factory and opened the door. Several rope workers looked up and acknowledged him with nods. Some didn't know he was a soldier, since he'd stopped wearing his uniform to work. But others knew and had resented him for taking a job from someone else. When he saw two of those men huddling in conversation, he regretted stopping. He hurried to the owner and explained his mission.

Garret Pine looked up from his ledger and laughed. "You want me to pay you money?" he asked.

"You owe me for a week's work," Tommy said.

"And what will you do if I don't pay?"

Tommy clenched and unclenched his fists. He knew he couldn't do anything. The owner would report him as a deserter. He now understood how foolish this trip had been. He had an urge to run, but didn't want to appear afraid. He forced himself to smile. He walked to the door, refusing to look to the right or left. When the door slammed shut behind him, he took a deep breath before racing away.

Once he was out of sight of the ropewalks, Tommy stopped. They might not like him, he assured himself, but they wouldn't do anything to hurt him. Besides, with the soldiers on Castle Island, he was safe. Tommy found those thoughts comforting as he made his way back to Will and Mr. Teasdale, who were deep in conversation.

But Tommy had not noticed one of the workers who had slipped out the back door and followed him to the meeting place. The man was careful to stay in the distance, but when he saw Tommy greet Will and Mr. Teasdale, he looked pleased. He studied their faces and watched as they loaded the wagon and headed out of town.

Then he went to the livery, where the wagon had been parked, and said, "I just saw a wagon and a few men. Who were they? They dropped this purse." He pulled his own money purse out of his pocket and held it up.

The liveryman scratched his head. "That was Teasdale. I guess the others were his hands."

"Where's their farm?"

"About two miles, Cambridge way."

"Good. I'll see they get this," the rope maker said, doing his best to hide a grin.

The ride home was a long one. The ice was no longer thick enough for crossing; so they had to circle around the Neck and take the ferry across the river, which added hours to the trip. As they traveled, Tommy and Will began to lay plans for their journey west.

"We should leave now," Will said.

"We could still have another snow or two," said Mr. Teasdale. "That would make traveling treacherous. You should wait until after the thaw and for the ground to dry."

"Where should we go?"

"Most people head for Connecticut or New York," Teasdale said. "Every spring a few families head off. Maybe one year I'll join them."

"Would they take us?"

"Sure, especially if they have no sons."

"But I know nothing about farming," Tommy said.

"We're strong and willing," said Will. "Besides, maybe we'll end up in a town that needs a press, and I could eventually own one."

Tommy grinned at Mr. Teasdale. "He's full of big ideas. You'll have to tell him that's not the way the world works."

"Why not? Many printers come from ordinary farming families. I don't see why Will couldn't do it if he is willing to work hard."

Even Will was surprised. "Really? You think I could do that?"

"Of course," Mr. Teasdale said. "If you don't do something foolish first."

SEVENTEEN

Slowly news trickled out to the farm from Boston. They heard that Captain Preston and some of his men had been arrested and thrown into jail. They heard that Sam Adams was using the massacre to drum up anger against the British up and down the Atlantic coast. Tensions increased, and the colonies drew one step closer to war. Then they heard that John Adams had agreed to defend the soldiers in court. He planned to blame the Boston mob for provoking them.

"How can two cousins, Sam and John Adams, see things so differently?" Tommy asked one April day.

"I don't know," Will admitted. "How can John Adams hope to stay and work in Boston if he successfully defends them? He'll make plenty of enemies. It's almost as though he's turned against his own people."

"He must think it the right thing to do."

Tommy began to relax. He no longer feared that red-coated soldiers would snatch him from the Teasdale farm. The young men worked hard to get ready for their trip. As the time for departure grew near, Will proposed a last trip to town.

"I don't have much, but Mr. Spelman gave me six leather-bound books that I think would fetch a fair price. I'll get much more in Boston than anywhere else."

"I'll come with you," Tommy said.

When Mr. Teasdale objected, Tommy said, "Nothing happened last time. I'll not do anything to draw attention to myself. I want to say good-bye to my uncle. I've written a letter for him to take to my mother and father."

"Will can take that for you."

Tommy's expression turned stubborn. "I want to do it myself. It's a small risk to take—and it is likely the last time I'll ever see my uncle, or any member of my family, again."

Mr. Teasdale agreed, and the boys set off. The road was still thick with mud from the spring rains, making it easier to trek cross-country than to try to follow the road into town. They had to wait an hour at the ferry, which carried them across the swollen river. Will fingered the leather satchel that hung at his side. Inside were the books he hoped would bring enough money for a rifle and other supplies.

"I hate being poor," he grumbled.

"I've never been anything else," Tommy laughed. "What would you do with more money?"

Will shrugged. "I don't know. But I hate reaching into my pocket and having so few coins to rub together."

In town they separated. Will headed for the bookseller, whom he knew through his last master, Mr. Mein. The man was a nosy fellow and a Tory; so Will was determined to say nothing about his reasons for selling the books.

When he entered the dusty shop, he found Mr. Boyd drinking a cup of tea.

"Well, if it isn't Will Northaway, patriot boy."

Mr. Boyd's weak jibe annoyed Will, but he put on a smile as he placed his leather satchel on the table.

"I'd like a price on these books," he said.

"Where'd you get them, lad?" Mr. Boyd opened the satchel and gently fingered the books. He set the leather-bound copy of *Foxe's Book of Martyrs* on the countertop, then examined the other books.

Though the man's face remained expressionless, Will could tell by the way he stroked the soft leather and thumbed through the pages that he wanted them. But would he pay?

The bookseller repeated his question. "Where'd you get these?"

"Mr. Spelman gave them to me before he sailed for England."

"Do you have any proof of that?" Mr. Boyd challenged Will.

"Proof? What do you mean? They were a gift. What kind of proof would I have?"

"You know as well as I do that I bought all your master's books. Mr. Mein had some fine ones—and these look as though they could have been part of his collection. If so, they belong to me."

As Will grasped Mr. Boyd's meaning, his face grew red. He grabbed for the books, but the bookseller was too quick for him. He pulled them out of Will's reach.

Will pleaded his case, but the bookseller merely took another sip of his tea and smiled. "I thank you for returning these to me," he said. "I won't press charges against you since you voluntarily came forward."

Will sputtered a protest. Before he could say anything more, Mr. Boyd added, "Oh, rumor has it that you have a deserter staying at the farm."

Will felt as though he'd been punched. "What do you mean?"

"You know what I mean," the bookseller said. "I'm guessing now that the roads are passable, a constable will be coming to arrest the lad. Too bad, for I hear he wasn't a bad fellow."

"Who told you this?" Will spat out the question.

"I guess he had the nerve to go to the rope factory and demand some back pay. You both suffer from the same ailment: greed. I never would have known you had my books if you hadn't come here demanding money for them. And the soldier, well, we know the mistake he made."

Will turned on his heel and stalked out of the shop. He was seething with anger and didn't know what to do. He couldn't believe that Tommy had been so foolish as to go to the rope factory—and made it worse by not telling anyone what he'd done. Will felt ready to wring his friend's neck, but first he had to find him.

With growing fear he searched for Tommy, realizing he didn't have a clue where to look. Finally he ended up at the Simpsons' house. Mr. Mattison wasn't there. Will hesitated a minute. He knew he wasn't supposed to tell Sam that Tommy had deserted. But Tommy had already put himself in danger. Will needed someone to talk to.

"You have to promise not to tell anyone what I'm going to tell you," he said.

"You can trust me," Sam said indignantly.

"The night of the massacre, Tommy deserted. He came out to the farm and has been staying there with us."

"You've known all that time and didn't tell me?"

"We didn't tell anyone except Mr. Mattison. But Tommy did a stupid thing. He's in town today, and there are some folks who know he deserted."

Then Will explained what had just happened at the bookseller's. Sam wanted to go immediately and get the books. Will urged patience.

"Where's Mr. Mattison?"

"He's getting the ship ready to sail," answered Sam. "We'll be leaving soon."

"Would Tommy be there?"

"Maybe. If he's on the ship he'd almost be in the shadow of Castle Island. It's kind of funny when you think about it."

Will shook his head. "I don't see the humor. If they catch him, they'll hang him."

"Let's go!" Sam looked regretfully around the kitchen. "We don't have many weapons here. My father's musket is so rusty it probably doesn't even shoot. I could take one of Mother's pans and hit someone with it if I had to."

Will brushed off his words impatiently. "We're not going to fight. We just want to get Tommy out of town."

Now it was Sam's turn to shake his head. "Ever since I've known you, you've been running from battle. One of these days you'll have to turn and fight. You can't expect everyone else to do the fighting for you."

Will scratched his head. "Come on, Sam. Let's find Tommy. We can argue later."

The boys left the house and headed for the dock. The closer they drew to the water, the more certain Will became that Tommy had probably gone in search of his uncle at the ship.

They passed by sail and rope factories until they came to a crowd near Long Wharf. Will tried to push through, but Sam was drawn to it.

"Wait," he said. "Let's see what's going on."

"We don't have time," Will hissed.

"It'll only take a minute." Sam strolled up to the crowd and pushed his way in. "What's going on?" he asked. Then his eyes settled on a figure lying crumpled in the street.

"What happened here?" Sam asked. "The fellow steal something?"

"He's a deserter. Some say he's one of the soldiers who took part in the massacre."

Will pushed his way into the crowd to the man lying on the ground. He stared at Tommy's bloodied face and looked back at Sam in dismay.

"Who will you turn him in to?" Sam asked the man who had spoken.

"We'll let the British sort it out," the man said. "He's one of theirs. We've sent a message to Castle Island. We'll watch him for two or three hours until an officer arrives."

Then Will had an idea. "I'll be back!" He mouthed the words to Sam before rushing down to the wharf. He prayed to find a waterman who would row him out to the *Ana Eliza*, and he prayed that Captain Mattison would be there.

He found a willing waterman and whispered his thanks as he silently urged the boat to go faster. The *Ana Eliza* was bustling with activity. He found Mr. Mattison in his cabin and quickly explained Tommy's predicament.

Mr. Mattison snapped into action. He removed a white wig from its stand and put it on. He changed into his best uniform and put on his best hat. Though he was not a soldier, a sea captain in uniform cut an imposing figure.

One of the ship's landing boats was lowered into the water. The captain, Will, and several frightening sailors with daggers in their scabbards boarded it. With several men rowing, it took only a short time to reach Long Wharf. Captain Mattison marched down, with his guard behind him. Will scrambled to keep up.

They strode to the rope factory, where they found Sam glancing anxiously around. His face sagged with relief when he saw the captain. "They've tied Tommy up. He looks pretty bad."

Mr. Mattison scowled and marched in the direction Sam was pointing. He found his nephew tied to a post, his head lolling to one side, his clothes torn and dirty.

"Who is in charge here?" he roared.

"I am." An apprentice came forward. "I'm watching him, though he's not going anywhere." He forced a nervous laugh.

"I'm Capt. John Mattison of the *Ana Eliza*, a British merchant ship. I consider it my duty to take him to the proper authorities. You may go."

The apprentice looked around uncertainly. The imposing figure standing before him said he was a captain. He was British. That seemed good enough.

Captain Mattison didn't wait for the boy to decide. He ordered his sailors to untie the ropes binding Tommy to the pole. They were halfway down the wharf when one of the rope workers came running up from behind.

"What are you doing? Where are you taking him?"

Captain Mattison pulled himself up to his full height and stared at the rope worker. The third sailor, who had dramatic tattoos on his face, stood alongside his captain. Will hid a smile behind his hand.

Without uttering a word, the captain turned and resumed his march to the boat. The sailor, Will, and Sam followed behind.

Only when they reached the craft and cast off from the wharf did Will relax. Now he had only to worry about his books.

EIGHTEEN

Tommy slept on and off for several hours. His nose was bloodied, and he'd taken hard kicks to the stomach and head. When he finally awoke and staggered to his feet, he groaned with pain.

Will had been waiting nearby with orders to bring him to the captain's cabin when he awoke. Tommy avoided his friend's eyes, but Will said nothing.

Captain Mattison was furious with his nephew. Once he knew that the boy was not seriously injured, he angrily rebuked him for his foolishness. Tommy hung his head. Finally Mr. Mattison stopped. He'd said everything there was to be said.

Only then did Tommy look up. "I'm sorry," he said. "I wasn't thinking. Please forgive me."

Mr. Mattison took a deep breath and nodded. "God protected you this time. It frightens me to think what might have happened. Now we have to decide what to do."

Will realized for the first time that their previous plan to go west would not work. Tommy couldn't risk going through Boston again. As they talked, a new plan took shape. Mr. Mattison would sail down the Atlantic coast and drop them off in New York or Baltimore. He had friends in both places.

Then Will explained about his books. "I should proba-

bly let them go," he said. "It's only money—though I have little enough of it."

"If Spelman meant you to have those books," Mr.
Mattison said, "you should have them. Mr. Boyd should not
be able to steal them."

"How can we prove they're his?" Tommy asked.

Everyone was quiet as they pondered the question. Then
Sam said, "Uncle William left several trunks at the house. I
wonder what's in them."

Will was eager to see what was in his old master's
trunks, but Mr. Mattison was leery about letting him go. He
had been seen with Tommy. Many people knew that Tommy
had stayed at the Teasdale farm. Will might find himself in
trouble. Instead, the captain urged Sam to go—and to take a
couple of his biggest sailors with him.

It took some searching, but Sam finally found his uncle's
ledger in the bottom of a trunk. In it were all the records of
his printing business. It recorded prices paid for paper and ink
over the years. It even noted when he took Will on as an
apprentice.

Sam continued to read. "I can't believe he wrote all this
down," he said, leafing through the pages. The last page contained a list of books. In the last column he'd noted how
he'd disposed of them. At the bottom of the page were listed
six books and next to them, in his uncle's distinctive hand-
writing, it said, *To Will Northaway, apprentice.*

Armed with the evidence, Sam marched over to Boyd's
with the sailors in tow. He demanded the books back. At
first the bookseller pretended not to know what Sam was

talking about. But when Sam pointed out the books on the shelves, Mr. Boyd changed his story. He claimed that he'd paid Will for the books.

That silenced Sam for a minute as he tried to figure out his next move. Then he thought about his uncle's meticulous accounts. He said, "Show me your ledger." It seemed obvious that businessmen wrote down every transaction in a book, just as his uncle had done.

Mr. Boyd hesitated, and Sam realized he'd won. The sailors stepped forward. One took his dagger out of its sheath and pretended to examine its long blade.

The bookseller's confident attitude wilted. "I must have erred," he said. "Let me pay you a good price for these books."

The other sailor said, "You'll pay twice the price. You've made difficulty for Will, and now you'll make—what's that word? Res-ti-tu-tion."

"Yes, restitution," the bookseller said nervously. "Giving what's deserved, and making up for the trouble. That's right." He counted out the coins. Sam put them in his pocket, enjoying the clinking sound.

Sam left the bookseller's and headed out to post letters that Will and Tommy had written to the Teasdales. It made the boys sad to think that they'd never see the kind farmer again. Or maybe they would. Only God knew the future.

Next Sam went home. He handed his mother the letter Will had written her. Then he packed his ditty bag, hugged his mother and brothers, slung the bag over his shoulder, and headed for the *Ana Eliza* without looking

back. He knew his mother would be watching, and he knew
if he saw her he might cry.

Mrs. Simpson watched her son until she could see him
no longer. Then she opened the letter from Will. He wrote
that he had come to Boston a near orphan. He was leaving six
years later like a son. Though her family and Will weren't
related by blood, they were by loyalty and affection. He
thanked her and thanked God.

Mrs. Simpson wondered what would become of him.
Unwritten in the letter, but much on all of their minds, was
the thought of war. No one knew when, but the Boston
Massacre had shown that it would come—maybe in a year or
two, maybe in five. At some point Will, Tommy, and Sam
would all have to choose whether and how to fight.

Will also was deep in thought as the *Ana Eliza* set out
from Boston Harbor. Maybe he was ready to go to sea again.
Maybe he'd work for a printer in New York. Maybe he'd go
further south. He did not know what would happen, but he
had a secure sense that he was in God's hands, and those
hands were strong and good. That night, as he climbed into
a hammock and felt it rock him as gently as a baby, he felt
at peace.